d Caregivers

aders are designed to provide en
experiences, as well as opportunities to develop
literacy skills, and comprehension. Here are a few ways to
support your beginning reader:

DISCARD

○ Talk with your child about the ideas addressed in the story.

○ Discuss each illustration, mentioning the characters, where
they are, and what they are doing.

○ Read with expression, pointing to each word. You may want to
read the whole story through and then revisit parts of the story
to ensure that the meanings of words or phrases are understood.

○ Talk about why the character did what he or she did and what
your child would do in that situation.

○ Help your child connect with characters and events in the story.

Remember, reading with your child should be fun, not forced.
Each moment spent reading with your child is a priceless
investment in his or her literacy life.

Gail Saunders-Smith, Ph.D.

STONE ARCH READERS

are published by Stone Arch Books, a Capstone Imprint
151 Good Counsel Drive, P.O. Box 669
Mankato, Minnesota 56002
www.capstonepub.com

Library of Congress Cataloging-in-Publication Data is available on the
Library of Congress website.
ISBN: 978-1-4342-2006-6 (library binding)
ISBN: 978-1-4342-2790-4 (paperback)

Summary: Gary the lizard and his parents have a fun day together.

Reading Consultants:
Gail Saunders-Smith, Ph.D.
Melinda Melton Crow, M.Ed.
Laurie K. Holland, Media Specialist

Art Director/Designer: Kay Fraser
Production Specialist: Michelle Biedscheid

illustrated by Andy Rowland

Little Lizard's
FAMILY FUN

by Melinda Melton Crow

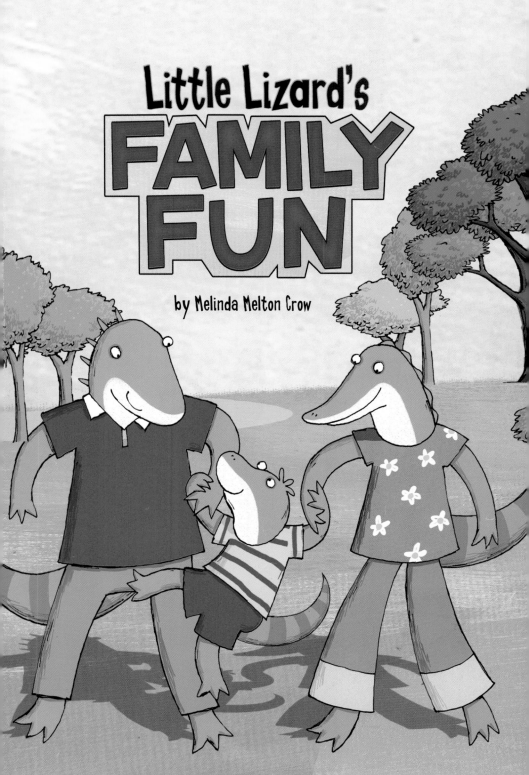

STONE ARCH BOOKS
a capstone imprint

This is Dad Lizard
This is Mom Lizard.
This is Gary Lizard.

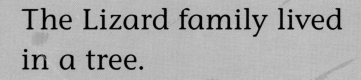

The Lizard family lived
in a tree.

Gary was little.
He liked to play.

"I like my slide," said Gary.

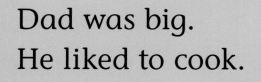

Dad's Recipes

Dad was big.
He liked to cook.

"Look at my cake,"
said Dad.

Mom was big, too.
She liked to garden.

"Look at my carrots,"
said Mom.

"May I have some cake?"
said Gary.

"Yes!" said Dad.

"May I have a carrot?"
said Gary.

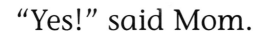

"Yes!" said Mom.

"Do you want to play on
my slide?" said Gary.

STORY WORDS

lizard	cook	carrots
Gary	cake	hooray
slide	garden	

Total Word Count: 93

Little Lizard's BOOKSTORE

STONE ARCH READERS — LEVEL 1
Little Lizard's **NEW BIKE**
by Melinda Melton Crow
Illustrated by Andy Rowland

STONE ARCH READERS — LEVEL 1
Little Lizard's **BIG PARTY**
by Melinda Melton Crow
Illustrated by Andy Rowland

STONE ARCH READERS — LEVEL 1
Little Lizard's **FIRST DAY**
Illustrated by Andy Rowland
by Melinda Melton Crow

4 NEW TITLES